The Case of the Baffling Beast

by Justine
and Ron Fontes

Illustrated by William Presing

The Case of the Baffling Beast is hand-illustrated by the
same Grade A Quality Jumbo artists who bring you
Disney's Doug, the television series.

New York

Original characters for "The Funnies" developed by
Jim Jinkins and Joe Aaron.

Printed in the United States of America.

3 5 7 9 10 8 6 4 2

The artwork for this book was prepared using pen and ink.

The text for this book is set in 13-point Leewood.

Library of Congress Catalog Card Number: 99-67853

ISBN 0-7868-4384-5

For more Disney Press fun, visit www.disneybooks.com

CONTENTS

THE CASE OF THE BAFFLING BEAST

BA-RINNNNG! BA-RINNNNG! The phone in the *Weekly Beebe* office jangled on the desk. "*Weekly Beebe*, Doug Funnie speaking." With all the eighth-grade staff members attending the Tri-County Future Paparazzi Convention, Doug was filling in as editor in chief, and Patti Mayonnaise was assisting him. He was hoping to put out a great issue, but there was one problem. Nothing was happening in Bluffington. Nothing at all.

"Hello, Douglas, my boy."

Doug recognized the voice of his

eccentric neighbor. "What is it, Mr. Dink?"

"Bigfoot was in my yard last night!" Mr. Dink said excitedly. "I've chosen you to bring my story to the people! Besides, *The Bluffington Gazette* wasn't interested."

"Bigfoot?!" Doug had seen "eye-witness" TV shows with choppy, blurred footage of a shaggy man-beast shambling through the woods. He figured if someone like that lived in Bluffington, he would have noticed. But as a reporter, it was his duty to check it out.

Besides, you never could tell . . . what if there really were a Bigfoot, and he and Patti found him? That would make him Doug Funnie, Ace Reporter. They'd probably make a TV movie about him, and maybe Patti would play his girlfriend. . . .

"We'll be right there," Doug said, hanging up the phone.

"Right where?" Patti asked.

"Mr. Dink's house. He says he saw Bigfoot in his backyard," Doug explained as he snatched up his notebook.

"Oh, really?" Patti chuckled. "Doug, there's no such thing as Bigfoot. Those stories are made up to scare people."

Doug coolly put his notebook into his pocket. "Well, I saw this TV show called *Mysterious Mysteries* that made me wonder if they're real," Doug replied. "Anyway, it's our duty as reporters to check out every lead."

"You're right, Doug," Patti said. "Let's go."

When they got to Mr. Dink's large pink house at 19 Jumbo Street, Mr. Dink was pacing up and down. "I'm so glad you're here!" he said, as Doug pulled out his notebook and flipped it open.

"What time did the Bigfoot encounter occur?"

Mr. Dink replied, "At 9:45 P.M. I heard my garbage can fall over. I checked my glow-in-the-dark watch. It speaks, too, you know. Very expensive. And sporty without being too athletic."

Doug nodded encouragingly.

"At first I thought it was the raccoons," Mr. Dink continued. "But when I ran outside, I saw a figure wobbling away on a bicycle. He had a large bag, like the paper boy carries, over his shoulder."

"Maybe it *was* the paper boy," Doug interrupted.

"Ah, yes, but he was hurrying like he

was running away from something," Mr. Dink continued. "Then I found some strange, oversized tracks on the ground, but they didn't lead anywhere.

"Now, my trash can is equipped with the latest in home security technology: an antitheft raccoon repeller with built-in video monitoring system. Very expensive. It repels raccoons without being insulting. And it looks great with my crush-resistant state-of-the-art garbage can with smell inhibitors."

"Mr. Dink?" Patti got right to the point. "May we see the tape?"

"Oh yes, of course."

Inside the Dinks' pink house, his wife, Tippy, was writing a speech for her next press conference. Mrs. Dink was the mayor of Bluffington.

While Mr. Dink fumbled with his expensive Numb-Your-Senses Entertainment Center ("entertains but never begs for attention"), Patti questioned Mrs. Dink. "Did you see Bigfoot, too?"

Mayor Tippy shook her head. "All I saw was someone riding away on a bicycle." She yawned. "Probably the paper boy. He had a big sack. Like Santa Claus."

"Santa Claus?" Doug muttered, shaking his head. "Don't tell me he's mixed up in this, too."

"There it is!" Mr. Dink exclaimed. Doug turned to the large TV screen.

"There *what* is?" Patti asked.

"I'll rewind it," Mr. Dink offered.

Doug watched closely as something large and hairy stomped in front of the

high-tech trash can. Mr. Dink was right. The raccoon repeller made a nice accent to the trash can.

"That could be anything," Patti said, squinting at the black-and-white blur.

"Including Bigfoot." Doug paused. "Or is it Bigfeet?"

Before going back to the office, the reporters questioned the other neighbors. No one else had seen Bigfoot or Santa Claus. One neighbor claimed to have seen the Easter Bunny, and he "looked like he was up to no good." Doug made a note but suspected the witness wasn't taking the investigation seriously.

Passing the town costume shop, Doug thought he noticed something different about the window. There was the usual giant beet costume and, of course, the Race Canyon outfit.

"Patti, do you notice anything unusual about the costume shop?" he asked.

Patti frowned. "I'm not sure," she said.

"Too bad the shop's not open yet or we could ask," said Doug.

They ran into Skunky Beaumont across the street from Swirly's. "Dudes, whoa. This place is way torque. First Bigfoot, and now you!"

"What was that?" asked Doug. "You saw Bigfoot?"

"You know, yeah, man. Big hairy dude, like, from TV! Whoa!" Skunky said.

Doug's heart pounded. A second sight-
ing! Could there really be a Bigfoot on the
loose in Bluffington?! And just when Doug
Funnie happened to be in charge of the
paper! His chest puffed with pride as he

imagined accepting his first Pulitzer Prize for journalism.

"Skunky, you saw Bigfoot right here in Swirly's parking lot?"

"Totally, dudes," Skunky said. "I wonder what he ordered."

Just then Doug saw Roger Klotz across the street in the parking lot in question. Doug and Patti hurried over to him. "Hey, Roger," Doug said. "Have you seen anything strange around here today?"

"Just you trying to play reporter," sneered the red-haired bully as he sauntered off, laughing.

On the ground behind where Roger had been, Patti noticed a cluster of Bigfoot tracks. "But they don't lead anywhere," she said.

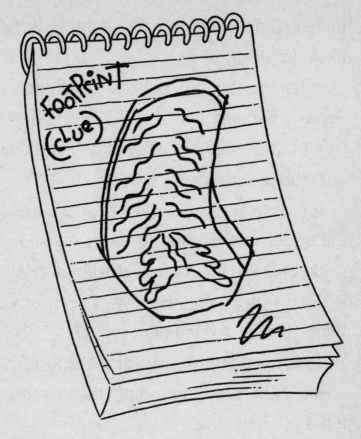

"That's just what I was thinking," said Doug. "It's just like the tracks at Mr. Dink's." Doug looked at the footprints more closely. "Hey, Patti," he said. "These footprints have strange markings in them." He pulled out his notebook and sketched.

"You're right," said Patti. "But what are they?"

Doug decided it was time to consult the experts. Al and Moo Sleech were experts on just about every strange thing Doug could think of. He was pretty sure they'd know all about Bigfoot.

Over at the Sleeches' house, Doug explained everything he and Patti had found out so far. "The tracks just stop," he said. "It's like something carried Bigfoot away—something big!"

The Sleeches had a private conference in code. Then they turned back to Doug. "The tracks stopped when the creature's spaceship picked him up," Al announced.

Patti's eyebrows went up. "What did you say?"

Moo continued. "The spaceship picked him up and carried him back to the Planet of the Bigfeet."

"So you *do* think these creatures exist?" Doug questioned. The Sleeches exchanged a glance.

"Twelve-seventeen," Moo said cryptically.

"Forty-six," Al corrected him.

"There's something else," said Doug, pulling out his notebook and showing them the sketch. "What do you make of these markings?"

Doug turned his notebook around to

show Al and Moo his drawing. As he looked at the sketch upside down, Doug made a discovery. "Hey, Patti," he said. "Do you suppose that Bigfoot shops at Shoes 'n' Shoes?"

"Very funny, Doug," said Patti. "Bigfoot wouldn't wear shoes."

"If he doesn't wear shoes," said Doug, "then why does he have the logo for Sky-AirJet sneakers in his footprints?"

"Two people in Bluffington saw Bigfoot on a bicycle," said Doug, flipping through his notebook. "But he wasn't delivering papers. Skunky saw him in the parking lot of Swirly's, but no Bigfoots were reported ordering a Frothy Goat or anything else. We find mysterious footprints, but they suddenly stop. And they carry the logo for Sky-AirJet sneakers, a sneaker so expensive that only Roger Klotz can afford them."

"But how could Roger be mistaken for Bigfoot?" asked Patti.

Doug and Patti looked at each other. "The costume shop!" they said at the same time.

Doug and Patti raced back to the costume shop. Roger's bicycle was already parked outside. Doug ran up to the counter just as Roger pulled a gorilla costume out

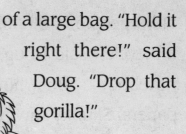

of a large bag. "Hold it right there!" said Doug. "Drop that gorilla!"

Roger tossed the gorilla costume over the counter. "You must be here to thank me, huh, Funnie?" He smirked. "Without me, you'd have nothing to put in your little newspaper."

Doug just shook his head. He had to admit Roger did have a point. Doug couldn't write the headline of his dreams— REPORTERS FIND BIGFOOT. But he still had a great story: REPORTERS EXPOSE BIGFOOT HOAX!

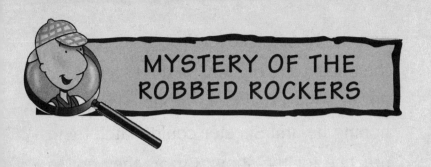

MYSTERY OF THE ROBBED ROCKERS

"I just got tickets to the Beets' Comeback Concert!" Doug exclaimed.

Doug's words made Skeeter honk with excitement. The Beets were the best group ever! At least, when they could stop arguing long enough to get through a song. "They're rehearsing at the con- cert hall right now. Want to go say hi?" Doug suggested.

The boys had

met the band on several occasions, since the Beets were big fans of the Psychedelic Fuzz, Doug's dad's old group. Doug was hoping he and Skeeter could watch them practice for the show. But as they got to the entrance, they saw a sign that read CONCERT CANCELED DUE TO LACK OF MEANINGFUL COMMUNICATION.

"Oh, no!" honked Skeeter. "The Beets have broken up again."

Just then the boys saw a man in a cavalry hat quietly close the back door of the theater and slip away. "Hey, isn't that Colonel Ketchup?" Doug whispered.

Skeeter honked softly. "But I thought they had a different manager now. Liz Grabbe. I read it in *Entertainment Hourly*."

Everyone had been shocked when the

Beets got a new manager. Colonel Ketchup had been with the band since the beginning. When they had their first hit, he presented them with a golden beet engraved with all their names on it: Munroe Yoder, Chap Lipman, Wendy Nespah, and Flounder. The band always said that the golden beet kept them together through it all.

Doug and Skeeter walked inside the concert hall just as a large roadie wheeled a cart full of sound equipment past them.

MUNROE YODER
CHAP LIPMAN
WENDY NESPAH
FLOUNDER

"No concert today, boys," the man said, shaking his head sadly. "Without the beet, there's no Beets."

Doug and Skeeter exchanged puzzled glances. "What does that mean?" asked Skeeter. Doug shrugged.

Suddenly, a woman in a red suit came clicking toward them on high heels, issuing commands into a cell phone. Doug recognized the band's new manager, Liz Grabbe.

"Get me a golden beet," she snapped into the phone. "The group won't go onstage without one. I don't know why.

You know these artistic types. Just get me a golden beet. No, a turnip is not acceptable. It has to be a beet." The woman snapped her cell phone shut and glared at Doug and Skeeter as she passed.

"Oh, no!" exclaimed Doug. "Not the golden beet!"

"Without the golden beet there is no Beets!" said Skeeter.

"We have to find it," Doug said. "It's our duty as detectives and as Beet fans." For an instant, Doug pictured himself striding forward shouting, "Seal the area! We have to keep the beet on the premises!" But then he and Skeeter were standing in front of the Beets' dressing room. They heard the sound of voices and pushed open the door.

"It was a lovely beet," keyboardist Wendy Nespah moaned.

"Remember when Colonel Ketchup gave it to us?" guitarist Munroe Yoder sighed. "That was brilliant."

"We shan't find another beet like that," said bassist Chap Lipman.

Flounder couldn't speak. He tapped out a sad rhythm on his drums. Then he looked up. "Hi, guys," he said to Doug and Skeeter. "Did you hear we've lost the beet?"

Doug nodded. "Skeeter and I are going to turn the beet around."

"Turn it upside down," Skeeter honked. The band tried to smile, but it was hard.

Just then Liz Grabbe jabbed her head into the dressing room. With one hand she covered her cell phone. "I've got a zucchini studded with cubic zirconium," she said.

"Sorry, ducks," Munroe said. "It's got to be the golden beet."

Liz harumphed and disappeared again.

"When was the last time you saw your beet?" Doug asked the band. "Where was it?"

"Chap had it last," Wendy announced. "He had it with him when he was rehearsing and smudged it up with fingerprints."

"That was yesterday," Chap shot back. "Anyone could have come in and nicked it since then. There's the maid. The janitor."

"I saw Wendy coming out of the beet room right before tea," Munroe said, eyeing Wendy suspiciously.

Flounder thumped his drum ominously.

Liz appeared again, cell phone in hand. "A fourteen-carat-gold-plated potato that looks a lot like a beet at the right angle. That's my final offer."

The band spoke in unison. "A golden *beet*, love! A golden *beet*!" Flounder hit the cymbals for emphasis.

"That's it," Liz said. "I'm out of here. I've got a plane to catch and six other bands dying for me to manage them." She turned to go.

33

"Um, excuse me, but maybe we can help you find the beet," Doug said. "Has anyone left since you noticed the beet was missing?"

"Hey, yeah," added Skeeter. "How do we know everyone's still here? The beet thief might already have beat it."

Suddenly, Doug snapped his fingers. "Wait a minute!" he cried. "I know who stole the golden beet!"

"We know the golden beet was in its usual spot yesterday when Wendy saw Chap getting fingerprints on it," Doug said. "But nobody saw it since before tea yesterday. None of the Beets have left the premises. Liz wouldn't have taken the golden beet because she could make more money if the band actually played."

"I certainly could," said Liz, her fingers itching to dial her cell phone.

"Who else knew how important the golden beet was to the band?" Doug asked.

"Only the four of us," said Flounder. "Oh, and of course, the—" He beat a drumroll, and stopped abruptly when the door opened and in walked—

"Colonel!" exclaimed everyone.

"Colonel, you've got the golden beet," said Wendy. "Wherever did you find it?"

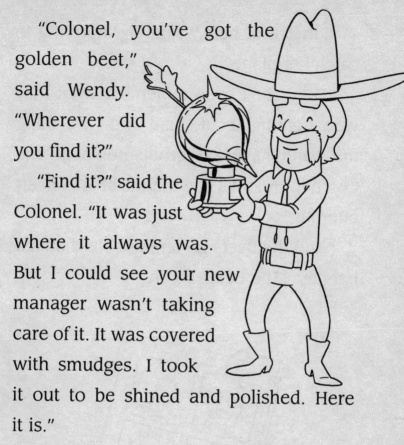

"Find it?" said the Colonel. "It was just where it always was. But I could see your new manager wasn't taking care of it. It was covered with smudges. I took it out to be shined and polished. Here it is."

The beet glowed beautifully in the dressing room light. The band broke into happy smiles. In a moment they were hugging.

"I'm out of here," said Liz, hurrying to catch her plane.

"They don't even remember what they were fighting about," said Doug, watching the band having a group hug with the Colonel. "It looks like there'll be a concert after all."

"And the Beets go on," Skeeter honked happily. "The Beets go on!"

THE LAST BOY ON EARTH

October was nearly over. Doug Funnie's family was enjoying what was probably the last picnic of the season in Mellon Point Park. Dirtbike was running across the grass. Theda and Phil were running after her, as they had been for most of the day. Doug was tossing a Wacky Wizzer with Porkchop, his best nonhuman friend.

Suddenly, Doug's sister Judy leaped in front of the Wizzer and shook a rattle at him. She was howling at the sky and wearing a big mask with antlers and feathers. Judy was a performance artist who attended the Moody School for the Gifted. She could get pretty weird, but this was odd, even for her. "What are you doing?" Doug asked.

Judy stopped howling long enough to catch her breath. "In the ancient Poulevian calendar, this is the Moon of the Others. The thirteenth Poulevian month. Wooohooo! Wooohooo!" Judy went back to howling.

Doug looked at Porkchop for an explanation. Porkchop shrugged his shoulders and made an "I don't know" noise. They looked back at Judy. "What does *that* mean?" Doug asked.

"Right now," Judy whispered, "the veil between worlds is thinnest. You never know what kind of creatures from other planets and worlds you might wake up—and find tomorrow. How do you think we got you?" Then she recited a poem of protection for Doug and Porkchop:

"May the sun that will rise
on all chickens and beasties
shine down and keep
these two little leasties.
Stay safe and warm,
walk in the light,
and don't be the main course
of anyone's feastie!"

Then she turned to Doug and said,
"You may not be much of a brother, but
you're the only one I have, and I might do
even worse if I tried for another. Here.
Take this chicken foot for protection," Judy
said. She handed him what looked like an
old sock filled with chewed bubble gum. It
smelled like cheese dipped in cough

syrup. Porkchop sniffed and backed away.

"Um, that's okay, Judy. Why don't you hold on to it? Porkchop and I aren't superstitious. The really good detectives never are."

Judy gave him a withering look. "You'll regret it, little brother, when strange creatures start to come after you," she warned. She leaped away, adjusting her antlers with one hand and shaking the primitive rattle with the other.

The afternoon flew by. It seemed almost too soon when the sun set. By the time they finished packing everything up, the Funnies were exhausted.

"Let's put everything away tomorrow," Theda suggested when they got home. Everyone quickly agreed.

"I'm turning in now." Judy yawned. Her feathers were drooping.

Theda said, "Me, too. I'm too tired to watch any TV." Phil agreed.

After everyone went upstairs, Doug and Porkchop settled down with one of their favorite videotapes, *The Last Man on Earth*. It was an old sci-fi movie about aliens who invade Earth by replacing

everyone with robots, except for the LAST MAN ON EARTH! It all starts when strange trucks start showing up carrying human-looking robots. The townspeople are replaced one by one until the hero is the only man left in an all-android world.

Doug's favorite scene was the one where the last man went to his best friend for help and it turned out he was already an android. The hero didn't know it until his friend's head started beeping. Then the android chased him down the highway in a truck with a mind of its own.

"Come on Porkchop," Doug said, as the last robot—a mechanical nurse—shorted out onscreen. "We've got to get up early tomorrow." He and Skeeter were meeting at the new Head-Over-Wheels Roller

Sports Course that had just been built at Lucky Duck Park. They wanted to practice skateboarding before it got crowded. Doug and his best human friend liked to practice without anyone around to laugh if they messed up.

Doug went upstairs to his room and set his alarm for six-thirty. He and Skeeter were meeting at seven. The half hour would be just enough time to throw on clothes, grab his skateboard, and get to Head-Over-Wheels.

BA-RIIIIIING!

Doug woke in his dim room, disoriented from dreaming. In his dream Doug was being chased by an evil ice cream truck shaped like a chicken that cackled at him

in a mad, robot-type voice: "Ba-bok! Come to the Great Chicken's Dinner! No one can serve you like we can! Bawk!" Doug was glad to wake up from that! The sky was barely light, but the clock showed 6:30.

Doug took a deep breath. "Why are we doing this?" he asked Porkchop groggily.

Porkchop flipped Doug's skateboard into his front paws.

Doug grinned. "Oh, yeah! Me and Skeeter are going to have Head-Over-Wheels all to ourselves!" Doug quickly dressed and he and Porkchop went downstairs.

Doug was surprised to find the kitchen deserted. The picnic basket was just where Mom had left it the evening before.

Doug checked the clock. It was quarter of seven. Even on weekends, his parents were usually in the kitchen by six-thirty. But the house was unnaturally quiet as he pulled the door shut behind him.

The sun was barely more than a bright sliver on the horizon outside and it was totally silent. Doug couldn't help looking around the empty streets for killer chicken ice cream trucks.

Doug jumped on the back of his skateboard and WHOOSHED down the deserted sidewalk. He had never been all alone on the street before.

"It's as if all of Bluffington has disappeared into nothingness," Doug exclaimed. "Except us."

Porkchop nodded.

SA-WOOSH! Doug swerved to a dramatic stop at the park entrance. Brittle leaves swirled under his wheels and crackled eerily.

Skeeter was nowhere in sight, but neither was anyone else. They still had plenty of time to practice alone. Doug wished the sun would come up.

Doug's watch read 7:05.

Doug decided to calm his nerves by practicing his moves while he waited. "Check this out, Porkchop!" Doug's voice echoed on the empty skateboard slope. Porkchop wasn't much of an audience; he kept dozing off.

Doug kept practicing, but Skeeter still didn't show. Suddenly Doug's stomach growled. He was getting hungry and

starting to really wonder about Skeeter. It was kind of creepy being at Head-Over-Wheels all alone.

He checked his watch: 7:15. "It's not like Skeeter to be this late—unless the robots got him," Doug joked to Porkchop.

Porkchop yawned.

"Okay," Doug said, "let's find a phone."

Doug soon found a pay phone near the doughnut shop, but as he was about to slide his phone card in, he jumped. A big Swirly Burger truck rumbled by. "Wait a minute," said Doug. "I've never seen a Swirly Burger truck before. Don't the burgers get made at Swirly's just like the Frothy Goats and Tater Twisties do? Uh-oh. What's really in the back of that truck?

I sure hope it's not a delivery of robots to take over Bluffington."

Porkchop rolled his eyes.

Just thinking about Tater Twisties made Doug even hungrier. "I know; that's silly," he said. "I just need something to eat."

Doug pulled on the doughnut shop's door, expecting to hear the bell jingle and Mr. Sleech's welcoming voice. The door didn't move. The sign on the doughnut shop's door read HOURS: 7 A.M. to 7 P.M.

Doug checked his watch again: 7:20. "Hey, Mr. Sleech," Doug called into the shop. "Time to make the doughnuts!"

Nobody answered. Doug felt a cold chill on his neck. The doughnut shop was *always* open on time. Maybe Mr. Sleech had been abducted by fried-dough-loving aliens and

his replacement robot hadn't shown up yet. Robots might not be very punctual. Skeeter's was twenty minutes late.

Another delivery truck rumbled by. Two trucks in five minutes! Doug thought. What factories were open on Sundays? And where were all the people?

Suddenly Doug saw a woman in a nurse's uniform walking to her car. Doug was so happy to see another human being that he started to take a step toward her. But when she got to her car Doug distinctly heard a high-pitched beep-beep-beep. "Oh, no! It's just like in the movie!" Doug said. The nurse's car door slid open with an ominous thud.

Doug thought of Judy's chicken foot and heard her warning in his head: *You'll*

regret it, little brother, when strange crea-
tures start to come after you.

"Let's get out of here!" Doug said. Porkchop nodded eagerly as they ran.

As Doug hurried home he wondered what would be waiting for him when he got there. Would it be his family—or only their robot husks? Would he be doomed forever to be THE LAST BOY ON EARTH?

Doug turned the corner onto Jumbo Street.

"Whoa! Careful, Douglas, my boy!" The voice sounded alarmed.

Doug ran right into Mr. Dink holding a big garbage can. At least it looked like his neighbor. It could be a robot coming for him!

Doug rushed into the kitchen and found his family all gathered around the breakfast table.

"Good morning, Doug! You're up early!" Theda gave her son a quick kiss. "Have a seat."

Slowly Doug sat down.

"Skeeter just called. He says he'll be about fifteen minutes late," Phil added.

Judy studied her brother's face. "You look like you've seen a ghost. Are you sure you don't want that chicken foot?"

"Wait a minute," Doug said. "This morning, the doughnut shop was closed past its opening time. We saw trucks making deliveries on Sunday. And, come to think of it, it would take longer than one night to replace an entire town's population with robots, even if you're an alien."

Doug looked from Judy to the kitchen clock and then down at his watch. He didn't need any chicken foot to know what was wrong. Doug slapped his forehead. "I should have known! It's standard time! Clocks get turned back one hour. It's only about six-thirty now! I just didn't remember the time change because we didn't watch TV last night. They would have said it on the news. We forgot to change the clock! And I forgot to change my watch!"

Suddenly Doug frowned. "But I still don't know where Swirly Burgers come from."

Doug Funnie sat in the library reading the last pages of *Smash Adams: The Man, The Mystery*. He had already read every Smash Adams comic and book, and seen the superspy's videos, twice! He had wanted to go to Bull's-eye Park with Porkchop today, but his dog was very busy.

Every year Porkchop's tepee won for Best Design or Art Collection in the annual Tri-County Tour of Dog Homes. It was no wonder. Although it looked like a simple tepee from outside, inside it was equipped with every possible convenience, from satellite TV to a bowling alley. This year Porkchop was adding a reflecting pool, which took up a lot of his time. So Doug was on his own.

Closing the book, Doug was amazed to see Roger Klotz in the library. It was not the bully's usual hangout.

"Hey, Roger!" Doug said. "Whatcha doing?"

Roger pressed the stack of books he was holding against his chest. Doug could just read the titles: *The Breeds of Tri-county*, *You Call That a Dog?*, *What Your Dog Says About You,* and *Finding Your Dog in the Stars: An Astrologer's Guide.*

"What's it to you, Funnie?" snarled Roger. "Can't a guy visit his local library without being hounded?"

Man, Doug thought as Roger rushed through the checkout desk and outside. What's eating him? And why's he taking out dog books, anyway? He has a cat. He hates dogs.

Doug knew what Smash Adams would do at a time like this. He would check it out. Roger Klotz was up to something, and knowing Roger that couldn't be good. Doug decided to investigate.

Doug slipped out of the library to follow Roger at a safe distance. Roger's next stop was Rose's Unisex Beauty Parlor for Men and Women, where his mother, Edwina, worked as a stylist. Doug ducked inside a doorway. In a moment, Roger came out carrying a book called *How to Make Wigs*.

"How to make wigs?" Doug said. He stepped back into the shadows as Roger passed by. As far as Doug could tell, Roger's red hair didn't seem to be thinning. Doug took out his detective's notebook and wrote: *No signs of male pattern baldness, yet reading about wig-making. Why?*

Next, Doug followed Roger to the needlepoint shop! He slipped inside and hid behind a display of Christmas stocking kits while Roger paid for his purchase.

"One yard of fine mesh," the clerk said as she rang up the sale.

Another puzzler. Why would Roger need needlepoint supplies? Doug wondered. Maybe Roger *was* losing his hair. He was so embarrassed he planned to stay home embroidering pillows rather than be laughed at. Doug didn't notice Patti Mayonnaise come up beside him.

"Hey, Doug! I didn't know you were into needlepoint!"

Doug nearly fainted at the sudden sight of Patti. "I . . . um, was just picking something up," he stammered, grabbing a kit off the rack.

"Advanced doily making?" Patti questioned, reading Doug's package. "Oh Doug, I didn't know you did doilies. And

ADVANCED
DOILY
MAKING
$7.95

you're advanced. That's amazing!"

"Uh, heh heh, um, well . . ." Doug muttered, wondering if anything like this ever happened to Smash Adams. As soon as Patti said good-bye, Doug left the store and hurried down the street. He could still see Roger heading up the block and he didn't want to lose him. He caught sight of him ducking into the Poofy Pup Grooming Salon. "Dog grooming salon?" Doug said. "Now this is really getting weird!"

While Doug was asking himself what Smash Adams would do now, Roger came out of the groomer's carrying a brown paper bag.

Doug ducked behind a mailbox just in time.

Roger's next stop was the Happy Tails Pet Shop. Roger almost spotted him there, but Doug cleverly stuck his head in a snake aquarium until Roger had paid for a dog collar and a leash.

Quickly, Doug unwound the snake that had wrapped itself around his face, completing his disguise. Then he hurried out of the store after Roger. He followed him

home to the Boogerton Heights mansion he and his mother shared. Roger went into the trailer that had been their original home and was now parked on the mansion's front lawn.

Doug peeked in the window. Roger put down the books and other strange things he'd gathered, and greeted his cat, Stinky. Then he flipped on the TV and settled down on the couch.

I guess that's about all the investigating I can do for now, Doug decided. He walked home, thinking over what he had seen: a dog-hater with dog books, a book about wig-making, a needlepoint net . . . None of it made any sense.

The next morning, Porkchop got Doug up early and they went to the dog show.

While Porkchop registered for the home decorating category, Doug took a walk around the mall. Who should be there but Roger, with a pet carrier. Doug peered through the steel-wired front.

"That's the weirdest dog I've ever seen!" he exclaimed.

"We're going to win for Most Unusual Breed," Roger said. "By the way, where's Cutlet?"

"That's Porkchop," Doug corrected. He took another look inside the carrier. The pieces were beginning to fall together. "I've got to go, Roger."

Just then, the dog arched its back and hissed!

Doug hurried as fast as he could over to the corner where Porkchop was being photographed right next to his new trophy for Best Dog House. "Come on, Porkchop!" he called. "Quick! We've gotta save the dog show!"

What kind of weird dog does Roger have inside the carrying case? And is that Roger's real hair?

Doug and Porkchop got to the dog show just as the Most Unusual Breed competition was being judged. Doug saw Roger standing beside his unusual pet. "Look, Porkchop," Doug said. "Roger's been reading up on exotic dog breeds. He's buying up craft supplies. He's studying the art of wig-making. He goes to Poofy Pup Grooming Salon with no dog and comes out with a suspicious package. Let's see what kind of dog this is."

Porkchop winked and walked over to Roger's new dog. Porkchop barked a greeting. Without warning, Roger's dog hissed loudly, arched its back, and leaped up on a pedestal. "I've never seen a dog that could do that," said one of the judges, scratching his head.

Down on the ground, Porkchop barked again. Roger's dog puffed up and off flew a homemade wig, a new dog collar, and two pounds of dog hair clippings. The cat underneath yowled at Porkchop and swiped her claw. Porkchop grinned.

"Disqualified!" shouted the judges.

"I knew it," said Doug. "Only Roger would try to win a dog show with a cat."

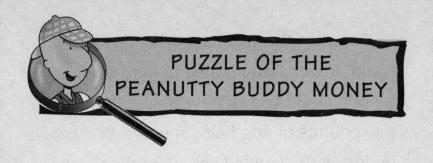

PUZZLE OF THE PEANUTTY BUDDY MONEY

The Swirly's ice cream truck jingle-jangled just outside the gate of Lucky Duck Park, surrounded by happy children. Doug saw Patti at the head of the line. Porkchop barked at Doug, dancing with joy. He raced for the truck, reaching for the money he kept in his fur as he ran.

"Oh boy, Peanutty Buddy time!" Doug grabbed his wallet and followed Porkchop to the truck.

"Hey, Doug!" Patti smiled. "Here for your daily Peanutty Buddy?"

Doug smiled back. He could practically taste the sweet peanutty buddiness. Then he heard Patti's cry of alarm. She was searching the pockets of her light blue pants.

"What's wrong?" Doug asked.

"My money is gone," Patti said. "I clearly remember putting ice cream money in my pocket, but now it's not there."

Doug said, "Do you have a hole in your pocket?" He had lost money that way himself and he hated to see it happen to Patti. She checked her pocket and shook her head sadly.

The girl of his dreams was in trouble! "Let me buy you one, Patti," Doug offered.

"Thanks, but no, thanks," she answered.

"I couldn't do that. Besides, I know I had the money this afternoon. Where could it be?"

"Don't worry, Patti. I'll solve this crime!" Doug declared, selflessly giving up his place in line. "Come on, Porkchop!" he said, grabbing Porkchop out of line, too.

Porkchop yelped, a stunned look on his face. He did not feel as selfless as Doug. He wanted his Peanutty Buddy!

Doug reassured him, "Don't worry, we'll get one later. As soon as we help Patti find her money." Porkchop grumbled, but he went along with his friend.

"That's awfully nice of you, Doug," Patti said. "But you should go ahead and get your own Peanutty Buddies. I know Porkchop wants one."

Doug's best nonhuman friend's ears perked up for an instant while he was filled with hope. But then Doug said, "Patti, we could never eat ice cream in front of you while you didn't have any! Could we, Porkchop?" For a second, Porkchop looked undecided. Doug urged him, "Porkchop?!"

Porkchop drooped as he looked at Doug with resignation in his eyes. He moaned pitifully and shook his head.

"Come on, Patti," Doug said. "We'll find your money or my name isn't Smash Ad— I mean, Doug Funnie!"

Patti laughed. "Okay, Detective Doug. What do we do?"

"We'll retrace your steps," Doug said.

With one last long look at the retreating Swirly's truck, Porkchop joined his friends. Doug patted his head. "Don't worry, boy. You'll get that Peanutty Buddy." Porkchop smiled bravely as they headed for Patti's apartment.

There Patti showed Doug a big pickle

jar full of coins. "I  save my change in here," she explained. "This morning I counted out enough for a Frozen YeeHaw Cluster."

Doug nodded. "Where did you go after you put the change in your pocket?"

"Well, I had breakfast with Dad," Patti said, leading the detectives to the kitchen.

"We talked about my birthday," Patti recalled. "Then I went to the mall with Beebe."

Doug checked the kitchen for places where Patti might have left the money. Nothing.

Doug, Porkchop, and Patti went to the mall.

"Did you spend any money here?" Doug asked.

Patti shook her head. "I'm saving for a new beetball glove I saw in the Jumbo Jox catalog."

"Where did you and Beebe go after that?"

Patti sighed. "That's when Beebe and I had a silly fight. Over a month ago I checked a book out of the library and lent it to Beebe. It was *Shop Talk: Mayors Discuss Politics*. She thought it was a guide to area stores. She said she returned it, but I just got a notice from the library that it's long overdue! It's my library card and . . ."

"I understand," Doug said, scribbling in his detective's notebook.

"Where did you go next?" he asked.

"I went home and ate lunch by myself," Patti recalled. "Then I went to the pool. I stopped to get my swimsuit and a clean towel in the laundry room."

"Aha!" Doug exclaimed. "Could you have left the change in the laundry room?"

Patti shook her head. "The change was in my pocket when I put my pants in my locker at the pool."

Doug, Porkchop, and Patti made their way to the public pool. They stopped outside the door to the locker rooms. "Tell me what happened next," Doug said. "Did you talk to anyone in the locker room?" he asked.

"Well, Beebe came in and put her bag down on the bench right next to mine. When I looked back Beebe was gone and *Shop Talk* was in my back-pack! I know it wasn't there when I packed for the swim."

Doug mulled over the information Patti had given him. "Where did you go after you left the pool?" he asked.

Patti smiled. "To the Swensens to baby-sit little Miles. I don't think he would take my money. He's more interested in shoelaces right now. He's two."

They walked over to the Swensens' house, passing Swirly's ice cream truck on the way. Porkchop moaned softly as he gave it a longing look. "So you and Miles just stayed at his house?" Doug asked as they approached the house.

"No, I took Miles to the park. We had a snack and . . . he spilled juice all over me!" Patti exclaimed joyously. "Doug, you're a genius!" She gave the baffled detective a fast high five.

"Come on!" she added. "Let's go get those Peanutty Buddies. I'll pay you back at home. I know where my money is!"

"What happened is—" Patti began to explain as they hurried after Swirly's truck.

"Wait!" said Doug. "Don't tell me. I think I already know what happened to your money. You put the money in your pants pocket this morning. You had it at the mall. After your fight, Beebe went home and found *Shop Talk* and slipped it into your bag. That's why she went to the public pool instead of using her own. She didn't take anything, she returned something. But then you went to the park with Miles and that's how you lost your money."

"Exactly," said Patti. "Miles spilled juice all over my pants, so I came home and changed them. But I never took the money out of the first pair I was wearing!"

"Porkchop, isn't that great?" said Doug. "Patti's got her money back!"

But Porkchop wasn't there. He was already in line for his Peanutty Buddy.

Have you solved all of the Funnie Mysteries?

The Funnie Mysteries #1:
Invasion of the Judy Snatchers
(0-7868-4382-9)

The Funnie Mysteries #2:
True Graffiti
(0-7868-4383-7)

The Funnie Mysteries #3:
The Case of the Baffling Beast
(0-7868-4384-5)

Each book contains 5 mysteries!

Available Now!